A Rookie reader®

S0-BOB-178

All Wrapped Up

Written by Thera S. Callahan
Illustrated by Mike Gordon

SCHOLASTIC INC.

New York   Toronto   London   Auckland   Sydney
Mexico City   New Delhi   Hong Kong   Buenos Aires

For Katie and Claire
—T.S.C.

Reading Consultants

Linda Cornwell
Literacy Specialist

Katharine A. Kane
Education Consultant
(Retired, San Diego County Office of Education and San Diego State University)

No part of this publication may be reproduced in whole or in part, or stored in a retrieval system, or transmitted in any form or by any means, electronic, mechanical, photocopying, recording, or otherwise, without written permission of the publisher. For information regarding permission, write to Permissions Department, Grolier Incorporated, a subsidiary of Scholastic Inc., 90 Old Sherman Turnpike, Danbury, CT 06816.

ISBN 0-516-24482-5

Copyright © 2003 by Scholastic Inc. Illustrations copyright © 2003 by Mike Gordon. All rights reserved. Published by Scholastic Inc., 557 Broadway, New York, NY 10012. A ROOKIE READER is a trademark and/or registered trademark of GROLIER PUBLISHING CO., INC. SCHOLASTIC and associated logos are trademarks and/or registered trademarks of Scholastic Inc.

12 11 10 9 8 7 6 5 4 3 2 1   4 5 6 7 8 9/0

Printed in the U.S.A.   61

First Scholastic printing, March 2004

It is Dad's birthday.

We have his gift,
but there is no tape.

We could use
gummy glue sticks,

7

8

or fluffy frosting,

or baby bandages,

11

or slippery syrup,

or gooey gum,

or mushy marshmallows,

or runny honey,

or sticky stamps,

21

or tacky taffy,

or jiggly jelly.

What would work best?
We did not know.

So we used a little of
this and a little of that.

And the paper stuck.

Word List (57 words)

a	his	sticks
all	honey	sticky
and	is	stuck
baby	it	syrup
bandages	jelly	tacky
best	jiggly	taffy
birthday	know	tape
but	little	that
could	marshmallows	the
Dad's	mushy	there
did	no	this
fluffy	not	up
frosting	of	use
gift	or	used
glue	paper	we
gooey	runny	what
gum	slippery	work
gummy	so	would
have	stamps	wrapped

About the Author

Thera S. Callahan lives with her family in Philadelphia, Pennsylvania. Her daughters, Katie and Claire, love doing arts and crafts and often use a lot of tape. Sometimes they run out. Their adventures in finding alternative sticky substances was the inspiration for this book. Thera has also written *Sara Joins the Circus* in the *A Rookie Reader* series.

About the Illustrator

Mike Gordon lives in sunny Santa Barbara, California, where he spends his days illustrating humorous books, greeting cards, and eating chocolate chip cookies with his two kids, Kim and Jay. Carl Gordon lives in England and worked on a computer to add the color to Mike's pictures for this book.